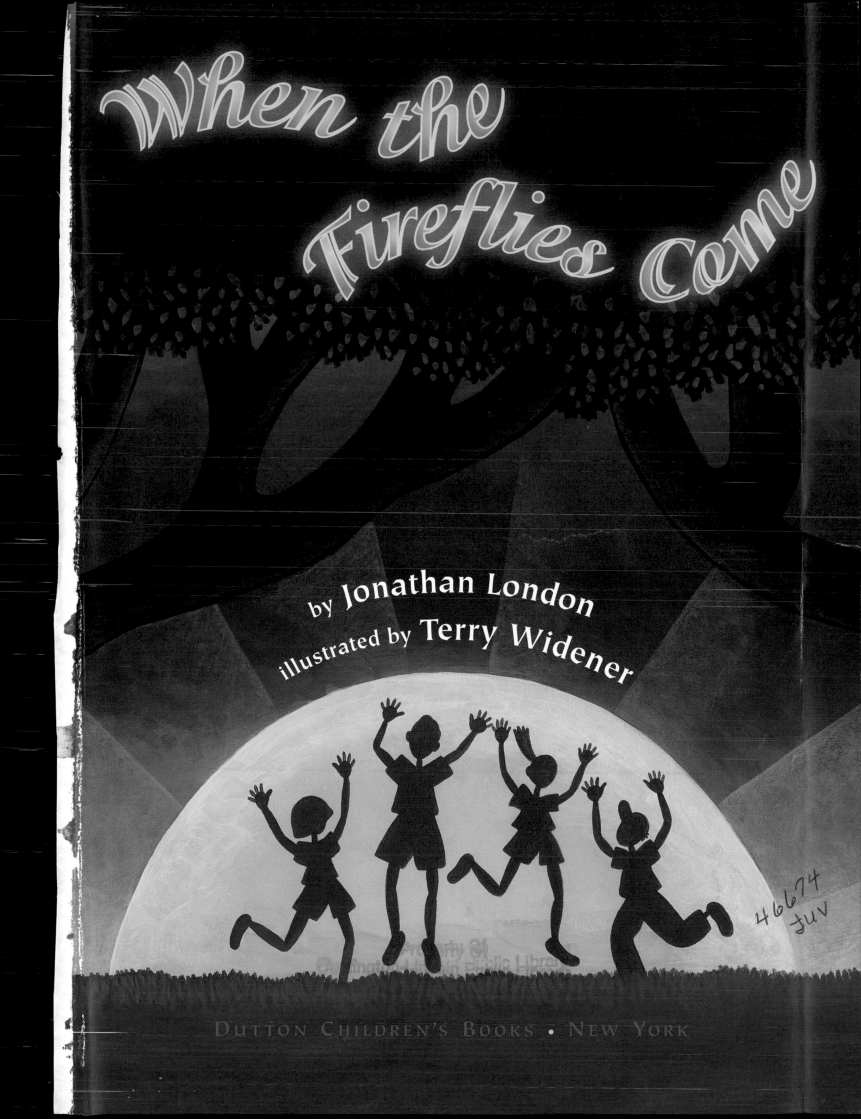

When the Fireflies Come

by Jonathan London

illustrated by Terry Widener

DUTTON CHILDREN'S BOOKS · NEW YORK

Text copyright © 2003 by Jonathan London
Illustrations copyright © 2003 by Terry Widener
All rights reserved.

CIP Data is available.

Published in the United States 2003 by Dutton Children's Books,
a division of Penguin Putnam Books for Young Readers
345 Hudson Street, New York, New York 10014
www.penguinputnam.com

Designed by Gloria Cheng

Manufactured in China
First Edition
10 9 8 7 6 5 4 3 2 1
ISBN 0-525-45404-7

For Michael and Claire,
who are living it now
—J.L.

For the kids I know who
love bugs
—T.W.

The screen doors slam. *Slam-bang. Slam-bang.* Outside, the smell of summer. The smell of fresh-picked corn, barbecued hot dogs and burgers in the air. The tinkle of ice in tall iced-tea glasses.

The *thong-thong* of backyard badminton.

The *slap-slap* of bare feet on the blacktop.

Bird chirp and bee buzz.

The *woof-woof* of a big dog at our heels.

Ching-a-ling. Ching-a-ling.

"Here comes the Ice Cream Man!" I shout.

Pennies, nickels, quarters, dimes—*ka-chink!*

Drumsticks, push-ups, and ice-cream sandwiches

melt down our chins and on our fists.

And off we run with sticky hands—me out front,

'cause I'm the fastest.

"Good-bye, Ice Cream Man!"

"Hey!" I shout. "Let's play ball!"

We grab our gloves and a bat.

We play ball in the field while the sun goes down. Our shadows are long; they run and jump with us. The grass is long and touched by the golden light.

Sammy, the pitcher, squints at me . . . winds up . . . and fires. *Pock!* Ah, the feel of a bat hitting a hardball to the outfield! *"Home run! Home run!"*

The fingers of night creep across the grass. The fingernail moon hangs low in the sky. The evening star dances beside it.

Still we play ball. An owl sails from his oak tree and enters the night. *Hoo-hoo-hoooo, hoo-hoo.*

Still we play ball. We play till it's too dark to see, fumbling shadows, tumbling in the soft air, rolling in the grass. Our backs get all itchy.

The score's 12–12 when I holler, "Called on accounta dark!"

When the fireflies come, it's time to rough-and-tumble. To leap and wrestle and giggle. To pile on top and pin down and tickle.

Grass fights!

The smell of torn summer grass on the warm night. Soft cries and loud squeals and laughter. *Hee-hee. Ho-ho.* "Oh no, that tickles!" Sammy cries.

"Say uncle," I say.

"Uncle!"

When the fireflies come, we become creatures of the night. We crouch and stalk and pounce. We play hide-and-seek and holler, *"Gotcha!"* I swing from the trees like an ape. *Hoo-hoo-hoo-hoo!* And we turn cartwheels in the stars.

Brahnk! Brahnk! A bullfrog booms from a nearby marsh. The crickets sing in the fireflies' light. *Cricket-cricket.*

When the fireflies come, we go after them. Tara runs
home to get jars for everyone. We chase and leap with
a jar in one hand and a lid in the other. Holes in the lid
for air. "Got one!" "Got one!"

Our jars are lanterns that blink. Off and on. On and
off. We're sending signals to the stars and the moon.

But the moon is going down now. The warm night breeze ruffles the grass. *Shhhh-shhhhh*. A bell rings. *Ting-a-ling. Ting-a-ling*. It's my mom. "Ah, darn. Time to go home."

Yellow light streams from kitchen windows and open doors. Moths flutter. Shadows lean in the grass and parents call.

"Sammy!"

"Tara!"

"Johnny!"

"Sue!"

Sammy starts to step into his house, hugging his jar of fireflies. I say, "*Look!* The stars are sending a message to the fireflies. They say, 'Come join us. Come spend the night!'"

I untwist the lid on my jar.

Sammy hesitates . . . then he and Tara and Sue untwist theirs—and we all hold up our jars to the night. The fireflies are *free!* They flit like sparks from a bonfire at a marshmallow roast. They dance and flash and bounce in the dark air, then disappear among the stars.

"Good night, fireflies!"

"See ya, Sammy!"

"See ya, Johnny!"

Screen doors slam. *Slam-bang. Slam-bang.*

In bed, I lie down in my shadow. My sheet is cool and my pillow as soft as owl feathers. The crickets sing in my window. *Cricket-cricket. Cricket-cricket.*

Summer is almost over. Sometimes it seems like the days come and go like the light of the fireflies.

Day-night. Day-night. Day-night.

An owl hoots. *Hoo-hoo-hoooo, hoo-hoo.*

I drift into sleep . . .